NICOLE

NICOLE

A NEW ADULT NOVELLA

Maren Hill

SANDPIPER PRESS

If you would like to know about new releases, giveaways, cover reveals, and personal stories, please sign up for my Newsletter:

WWW.MARENHILL.COM

I'd love to have you on board.

CONTENTS

JUNE 13, 1952, MAPLETON, ONTARIO, CANADA

As Sadie pushed her baby pram across the green lawn at the church social, she could hear the happy chatter of families seated at the picnic tables scattered about the area. Almost everyone in the church community came out every year, and people looked forward to the traditional offerings of the cold supper. Potato salad; fresh ham, turkey, and roast beef from local farms; orange jellied salads with chunks of pineapple inside; Jessie's homemade buns, and homemade pies of every kind were spread out on long buffet-style tables so people could keep coming back for more.

The early evening was warm, the air still, with the sweet fragrance of peonies blooming in the rectory garden. Mellow tones of the tenor sax could be heard as the band began tuning up their instruments in preparation for the dance, the large wooden dance floor having been put in place that very morning.

"Izzy, I have to use the ladies' room; do you think you could hold Nicole for me?" Izzy and Sadie were life-long friends, having grown up together and attended the same schools.

"Oh, I'd love to hold your newborn, Sadie! She's adorable," and Izzy began a high-pitched, one-sided conversation as she bounced Nicole up and down, up and down. "Aren't you just the cutest baby in the whole wide world? Yes, you are! Yes, you are!"

Making her way to the church hall, Sadie opened the door

to the ladies' room and could hear a conversation between two women in the other two stalls. Finding one stall still available, she opened that door and, as she sat down on the toilet, the conversation continued.

"I hope she'll be a better mother than her sister turned out to be."

"Yes. We're running out of mothers who're willing to take in strays." Sadie could hear the two women snickering.

This conversation was nothing new to Sadie; she knew she'd never outlive the shame. Her older sister Margie had earned a reputation as a runaround, flaunting her sexual prowess among the men, but not taking responsibility for any of the children born of Margie's frivolous liaisons.

Sadie had made it her mission to show the world that she was different from her wayward sister, and that started with never speaking to Margie again after her third child was born. Margie had moved in with her latest conquest without her newborn and, of course, without her other two children who'd been mercifully taken in by other parents in the community. Sadie understood that accidents happen; it was what happened after the accidents that threw the family into a state of disgrace that promised never to be forgiven in that small rural town of the fifties.

It was said that the latest baby slept in a dresser drawer at her grandmother's house until volunteer parents came forward to take on the child's upbringing.

"How many were there, anyway?" asked one.

"Let me see," the other said, and Sadie imagined her using her fingers to count. "Timothy went to the Jacks; Raymond, to the Smiths; Allan to the Orrs; Henry to the Masons; and the twins, well, Margie's mother took them in."

"Six kids! And Margie didn't raise any one of them herself."

"No, I guess she had better things to do like hunt animals and men. She's a trophy hunter, they say," and the women snickered again.

Sadie had learned to turn a deaf ear to disapproving women and do her best to get on with her own life and raise her daughter Nicole to be nothing at all like her Aunt Margie. For Sadie, it was a matter of survival.

Sadie was a single mom, her husband Dennis having been killed by a train when his wheelchair got stuck in the tracks only a month before Nicole was born. That devastating tragedy wasn't the first during their short, married life together, as Dennis had been shot in a hunting accident during Sadie's first trimester.

Dennis had been thrilled when he learned that Sadie was pregnant. Being from a family with eight children, he'd hoped they'd have at least four of their own. Knowing that he was infertile after the shooting, the prospect of a new baby became even more precious to Dennis.

Dennis had tried to be as independent as possible in spite of the severity of his injuries from the shooting accident. One day, as he'd crossed the railroad tracks that ran through their small town, his wheelchair had gotten stuck as a train came barreling towards him. Despite frantic efforts of onlookers to reach Dennis, it was too late.

As Sadie tried to absorb the shock of losing her husband, she began to question why she'd wanted a baby in the first place. It was mostly for Dennis.

She brooded about the future, knowing that her baby would grow up without a father. It would be up to Sadie alone to instill values, enforce rules, provide love and support, help build self-confidence, be a strong role-model. And then there was the matter of finances. Sadie didn't know how they would survive.

If the baby turned out to be a girl, well, that was definitely not Sadie's preference. She'd seen first-hand how much trouble a female of child-bearing age can get into, and how the consequences can be far-reaching. In her prayers, she'd asked for a boy.

Sadie's own father had been a model of respect and kindness towards Sadie and females in general, providing Sadie with confidence and a feeling of self-worth. *If I have a girl, she will not have a father to show her who she is and to teach her what men are like.*

COCOON

THE SIGNATURE ORANGE-AND-WHITE DIAGONAL STRIPES ON THE engine of the CP Rail train that would carry Nicole from Toronto to Vancouver on Friday, June 26, 1970, reminded her of a flag welcoming her to a new world. Finding the coach seat beside her vacant, she adjusted the reclining armchair and headrest then stretched out her long legs to rest her feet on the footrest.

She reached into her bag to retrieve a warm blanket. Cocooning herself against the world she was about to leave behind, Nicole closed her eyes and relaxed into the recliner as the train pulled away from the station.

Her mind began to wander, and she thought of how rigid her mother had seemed, there in the train station, saying goodbye to her only child, not offering any hug or other show of affection. But Nicole was used to that.

"Goodbye, Nicole. Let me know when you get in." Nicole watched as Sadie turned and walked away.

Nicole's mind wandered to her eight-year-old self and a day she'd never forget. All the mothers had come to the town hall to see their daughters off to summer camp. Excitement filled the room with happy chatter, and Nicole watched as mothers hugged their children goodbye; some even said "I love you."

But Sadie had been sullen that day, for reasons unknown to Nicole. When her mother put down Nicole's suitcase and said,

"Goodbye, Nicole; I'll pick you up next Sunday. Have a good time," and turned and walked out of the building, Nicole felt the hurt deep inside her soul. She no longer looked forward to going to camp, but she didn't want to go home either. It was hard to hide her disappointment and shame from her happy friends and, when one of them asked her, "What's wrong, Nikki?", all she could think of saying was, "I don't feel well."

Nicole's mind drifted to Mitch, her one true love. They'd started dating when she was in Grade 10 and he in Grade 12. She was the envy of her girlfriends. "He's built," they would proclaim as they admired his long legs, slender hips, flat belly and bulging biceps.

"He's easily the most handsome guy in the whole school." With thick black hair upswept at the forehead, Elvis style, and sapphire blue eyes, he could have any girl he wanted. But he chose Nicole.

Nicole thought about the fun they'd had only a few weeks before at Pinecrest, a dance hall for teens. She and Mitch had found a spot on the crowded floor and stayed there through most of the night, with Mitch popping outside at times to join others in sharing a mickey of vodka.

CCR's "Bad Moon Rising", The Rolling Stone's "Honkey Tonk Women", and Sly and the Family Stone's "Hot Fun in the Summertime" sent them rocking.

They were both covered in perspiration from the warm summer night, the crowd, and the energetic dance moves. And when Elvis Presley's "Can't Help Falling in Love with You" came on, she melted into Mitch's strong upper body, placing her head on his shoulder. Cuddling up to him made Nicole disappear into another world, a world where she felt loved, comforted, and understood.

They'd stretched out in a farmer's field on that sultry June evening, not even thinking about the possibility of mosquitoes and other flying insects. Knowing that they wouldn't see each other for maybe half a year lent a level of intensity that was hard to bear.

"Mitch, please try to look at it this way. We would have been apart anyway, with you off to U of T to finish your degree. It's the perfect opportunity, really, to go out on my own and see what this life might hold in store for me."

"So, this life isn't good enough then, Nikki?" Mitch's tone was a mixture of hurt and anger.

"In some ways, it's perfect, Mitch, and that would be the part involving you." She tenderly swept her fingers across the left side of his jaw.

Mitch turned away. "So, as perfect as we are together, you're willing to set that aside and explore other possible options that may or may not be there, is that right?" He'd raised his voice and now looked sternly into her eyes, putting her on the defensive.

"Look, I just turned 18. I've lived in a small town all my life, and have been the subject of ridicule from small-town gossipers. I grew up with no father, and I was raised by a mother who never really wanted me." Nicole clenched her teeth, and her eyes filled with tears.

"Ridicule? What're you talking about, Nikki?"

"Come on, Mitch; you can't pretend that you haven't heard the rumors."

"What? You mean when people chant that stupid 'First comes love, then comes marriage; then comes Nicole with the baby carriage?' That one?" Mitch looked incredulous to think that such teasing could have affected Nicole to such a degree as to cause her to want to leave town.

"You obviously never understood the reasons behind their meanness. And you obviously don't know what it feels like to be ridiculed." Nicole hung her head in shame.

"Are you talking about your aunt?" Mitch lowered his chin and drew his head back, staring into Nicole's eyes. "You can't be serious! You are not your aunt!" Mitch strongly emphasized the last five words. "And who cares what those idiots think, anyway?" He placed his hands on either side of her head and drew her head towards him so that they were eye-to-eye.

"Now, you listen to me. You're about as pure and honest and, I don't know, worthy of a person as anyone could possibly be. You're my girl, and I know how to pick 'em, Baby. You're the real deal."

Nicole drew back a bit, not wanting to be flattered or convinced to change her mind. "I know how you feel about me, Mitch; I'm not worried about that. But I feel stifled here in Mapleton. Same people, same opinions, nothing ever changes."

"Then move to Toronto, not 3000 miles away to Vancouver!"

"Sure, I could do that, but we'd be back and forth to Mapleton 'cause both our parents are there. I don't want to be under the influence of my mother or of the petty, small-town thinking that makes me feel bad. Mapleton's a dead-end street."

"Nikki, I know you're a hard worker, and I know you have your sights set on greater things, why wouldn't you?" He stroked the side of her head, lifting her hair behind her ear.

"Mitch, you've lived in Toronto and are headed towards engineering. Can't you see that I need to find my own way? Don't you think I owe it to myself to move ahead in life like you have?" By now, Nicole's voice had risen a few decibels.

"I get it, Nikki. Your upbringing was harsh, you need to 'find yourself'. But here's the part I don't get. We've been committed to each other for two full years now, we've sworn our love for each other up and down and sideways. And you want to abandon all that while you go 'find' yourself?"

"Okay, I guess I couldn't expect you to understand, Mitch." Nicole stood up, tears of frustration and sadness in her eyes. She turned and walked towards the dirt road.

Mitch sat for a moment then got up and followed her. "Nikki, don't get all upset. Come here, Babe." He caught up to her and drew her in with his strong arms. She allowed him to envelope her, but didn't return the hug.

"You dated several women before we met, but you're the only man I've ever dated. Think of that, Mitch, I haven't known any man other than you. And, even though I love you to bits, I don't want to spend the rest of my life wondering what it might have been like…"

"Yeah, Baby, I see what you mean, I guess." He paused as Nicole wrapped her arms around his shoulders as she waited for him to continue. "It doesn't make it any easier, though." Mitch's voice was soft in the quiet evening lit by a thousand stars.

"And, of course, Mitch, I'd understand if you wanted to date others while I'm away; I mean, that's only fair, I guess." Nicole tried to keep from crying, but tears ran down her face. As she pressed her cheek against his, she felt at one with Mitch in spite of their struggles.

With their arms around each other, they returned to their spot in the field. "Mm-hmm. Yeah, Nicole; if you and I are meant to be, then I guess we will be." He gently raised her chin and pressed his soft, wet lips against hers.

Nicole enveloped him in a warm embrace and melted her lips into his as they rolled sideways onto the plaid blanket. Blending one into the other felt as natural as burning hot candle wax pooling at the top of the candle.

Lost in each other for those precious moments, Nicole felt as though she was standing at the centre of the universe until she was rudely jerked out of her dream-like state by the sting of a mosquito bite on her bare leg.

"Oh, they're all over the place," said Mitch, as he began scratching his shoulder.

In a way, Nicole was glad that their passion had been interrupted because it was already starting to gnaw away at her resolve.

Nicole opened her eyes as a man in a business suit made his way down the aisle past her seat. Leaving Mitch behind, Nicole knew, was like leaving a part of herself behind. She knew she'd likely have to remind herself from time to time of her reasons for leaving. *Why does life have to be so hard?*

Nicole took a walk to the back of the train to the viewing car. There, with the breathtaking Canadian landscape displayed in a panoramic view, Nicole allowed herself a bit of excitement for what might lie ahead.

BEGINNINGS

THE SOUND OF NICOLE'S FOOTSTEPS AS SHE WALKED ACROSS THE marble floor at Pacific Central Station in Vancouver joined the hum of people coming and going at ten a.m. on the 29th of June. Nicole used the pay phone and treated herself to a taxi for the short, 15-minute drive to her apartment on Haro Street.

"The Elaine on Haro, please." Nicole reminded herself of a smart, confident woman she once saw in a movie when she said those words. Proud of herself for getting this far, her excitement rose as she spotted the light pink stucco apartment building bordered by shrubbery and fronted by a green lawn and a paved walkway. She paid the fare, grabbed her two suitcases, and stepped out of the cab.

Right inside the front door on the left, she knocked on Apartment 100 and collected her key from the landlord. Heading up to the third floor of the three-story walk-up, she smiled to herself, pleased that she had chosen an apartment close to Stanley Park to the north, English Bay to the west, and Vancouver Harbour to the east, even though she couldn't actually see any of those things from the second floor. Land-locked Mapleton, Ontario, seemed closed and stifling, compared to this new world surrounded by water and mountains. Finding Apartment 304 down the hall to the right, Nicole set her suitcases down on the floor and turned the key in the lock. Inside, the furnished apartment smelled of fresh paint. The parquet floors were devoid of area rugs or any other carpeting, the walls bare. She brought her suitcases in, locked the door, and looked around.

Going directly to the west-facing windows, she gazed at the city in the late afternoon light, full of wonder at what adventures awaited her. She sat down on the moss-green chesterfield sofa and stretched out her legs, resting her feet on the walnut coffee table in front of her. Two-tiered end tables flanked the sofa, and a television set supported by a walnut cabinet stood to the left of the front window. A vinyl lounge chair was positioned off to the left, for easy viewing of the tv set.

The kitchen appliances were white, the Formica countertops pink, and the solid wood kitchen cabinets had a reddish hue. The small kitchen wasn't exactly what Nicole had dreamed of, but at least it was hers, and she could make it more her own as time went on.

The queen-sized bed seemed luxurious to Nicole, who'd slept in a single bed her entire life. A green quilted bedspread comple-mented the headboard, which had a fabric inlay. The walls were painted a gold colour, and the floor-length curtains were off-white. Tall white lamps majestically crowned the bedside tables. Nicole couldn't wait to settle in for the night.

When she pushed open the door to the walk-in closet with built-in shelves, Nicole quickly inhaled as her lower jaw dropped open. Only in magazines had she seen a walk-in closet and, as far as she knew, none of the people in her rural community in Mapleton had such a thing in their homes. She dreamed of one day having enough clothes, shoes, and handbags to fill the lux-urious space.

Even though she was well aware that it was a huge stretch to rent this place, she also knew that she'd wanted to give herself her best chance to like Vancouver, and to want to stay and make it on her own. The money she'd saved over three years, working every summer plus weekends and evenings during school, wouldn't pay the rent beyond the next few months. She had to find a job.

Nicole's gurgling tummy reminded her that she needed to find some food. Checking the yellow pages of the phone directory, she saw that there was a deli nearby, so she headed out onto the lit street.

Monday at seven p.m. was alive with the sounds and movement of people coming and going on foot and in motor vehicles; Nicole felt excited to experience the energy of the waterfront city at night. The corner store deli was only two blocks away, and she picked up a smoked meat sandwich and cola, with a piece of lemon meringue pie for dessert. Spotting the July edition of Vogue in the magazine rack, she made sure she had enough cash before adding it to her purchases.

Arriving back at her apartment, Nicole put the key in the door lock and turned it. As she entered the kitchen, setting her makeshift dinner down on the counter, she mused that it would likely take some time before she fully realized she was now a resident of Vancouver.

Turning out the bedside lamp, Nicole settled under the sheets and listened to the sounds of the city. The unfamiliar noise of traffic, with horns blowing and sirens screaming, intermingled with the shouts of street revellers far into the evening made her feel uneasy. After tossing and turning for half an hour, she thought of calling Mitch, in spite of the cost of a long-distance call. Remembering the three-hour time difference in Ontario, she realized she was stuck. Too late to call, too late to go out anywhere by herself. Despite the liveliness outside her window, Nicole experienced a strange and uncomfortable silence within.

INVISIBLE

AFTER A RESTLESS FIRST NIGHT IN HER NEW APARTMENT, NICOLE decided to call her mother. "Hi Mom; I just wanted to let you know that I arrived safely and am just getting settled into my apartment."

Silence greeted Nicole on the other end of the line. Then, as if kick-started by some unknown force, "I'm so glad you called, Nicole. I was worried."

"Nothing to worry about, Mom; I'm 18 now, not your little girl anymore."

Another pause, this time longer. Feeling the awkwardness of the conversation, Nicole was about to change the subject.

"No, I suppose not, Nicole. You're on your own, really, now that you've left home." Nicole wasn't sure if her mother was admonishing her. She thought for a moment before replying.

"That's right, Mom; you're not responsible for me anymore. I hope you'll go have some fun. I really do."

Nicole cut the call short, wanting to find a place to buy groceries, garbage bags, paper towels, toilet paper, and some cleaning supplies.

With a fully-stocked fridge and enough supplies to keep her going for a week and longer, Nicole decided to explore her surroundings. In the foyer of The Elaine, Nicole noticed a woman about her age fumbling with her mailbox key.

"Oh, hi neighbour. I'm Nicole; I just moved in, so thought I'd introduce myself."

The young woman reacted as though Nicole was interrupting her mission to get the mail. "Hi. This stupid key gives me so much flack!" and she continued struggling a moment longer when the latch finally opened. Collecting her mail, she slammed the mailbox door shut, locked it, and turned to Nicole.

"I'm Colleen. Welcome aboard." And she headed down the hallway, seemingly to her apartment on the first floor.

The next day, July 1, would be Canada Day, and the red-and-white Canadian flag was displayed in shop windows, strung across balconies, and flown atop office buildings. The streets were crowded with people enjoying the warmth of a sunny Tuesday afternoon.

Greasy spoon diners made up a good part of the restaurants around town and, at night, they were brightened by the glow of neon lights.

In the warm afternoon, Nicole's throat felt dry. Making her way through a group of young people wearing checkered pants, leather jackets, blue jeans, and smoking cigarettes, she popped into a small shop beside the Hotel Broadway and bought an Orange Crush. No one paid any attention to her.

Back on the street, Nicole surveyed the scene once more. A sign for The Kit Kat Klub pictured a woman in tight pants and a top with spaghetti straps; her long black hair hung loose as she was depicted in a sitting position, knees bent to one side, and her long, bare arms stretched back to show off her chest. Nicole was curious about what went on in places like that.

Other signs advertised sauna baths, hotels, Chinese food restaurants. Some of the streets seemed dirty and unappealing, with the odour of garbage and urine. Surrounded by so much natural beauty, those streets marred the image that Nicole held in her mind as the otherwise perfect city by the sea.

"Hey, Beautiful, can I buy you a drink?" A light tap on her right arm had alerted Nicole that a blonde-haired man with striking grey-green eyes was wanting to connect with her. His strong, fit body probably made his ordinary blue-jeans and tee-shirt look sexier than they ordinarily would.

Nicole wouldn't be of age until next June. She'd heard about nightclubs such as Starvin' Marvins but laughed out loud when she read in a visitor's guide about Frank Baker's Attic in West Vancouver. Apparently, the ladies' washroom had a replica of the statue of David complete with a fig leaf that could be lifted. Unknown to the woman who lifted the leaf, a bell would sound in the bar with each lift, announcing that someone had been curious. The bell could not be heard in the washroom, so the curious might well wonder why some patrons were laughing and pointing at her as she walked back into the bar.

"Oh, hi!" Nicole's eyes widened, and her pleasure at being called "Beautiful" was easily seen in her smiling eyes.

"I take it that's a 'yes'?"

Charmed by his humour and surprised by her own response to a complete stranger, she wanted to keep him interested. "You know, I'd take you up on that but, to be honest, I don't turn 19 until next year."

He leaned in as though conspiring with her, "And no false i.d., I gather?"

"Uh, no, that sounds like it's maybe against the law?"

"You know what I think, sweetheart? You should be against the law for being so sweet and innocent."

Nicole didn't really want to come across as being naïve, but her circumstance didn't seem to matter to him anyway.

"I'm Mark, by the way. Are you from around here....ah, what's your name?"

"I'm Nicole and, no, I'm from Ontario."

Mark seemed inspired. "Come on, then, how 'bout I show you around the town?" She held his arm as they strolled about town, and it felt good to Nicole to have a companion in an unfamiliar city.

They stopped to view over a hundred pleasure boats moored along five rows of docks in the harbour while more were scattered throughout the bay. A density of tall office buildings enhanced by deciduous trees and green lawns stood majestically in front of a backdrop of mountains. *Vancouver must be one of the most beautiful cities in the world. I need to figure out a way to stay here.*

Turning onto Granville Street, and looking at the historic Orpheum sign in theatre row, their attention was drawn to a group of protestors walking on the street, led by a guitar-strumming demonstrator. Nicole read one of the placards, "End the War in Vietnam".

Nicole learned that Mark worked as a logger, living in logging camps much of the year. With the approach of sunset, she began to feel fatigue following her restless night.

"Thank you for showing me around, Mark, but I think I'm feeling the effects of a different time zone, so I'm going to call it a night."

"Do you mind if I call you sometime, Nicole?"

She dug deep into her resolve to meet new people and explore big city life even though she was missing Mitch. "Sure," she offered, reaching for a pen and the memo pad she carried in her purse. As she jotted down the number, Mark leaned in and kissed her cheek, then swept her hair behind her right ear. Nicole tore the page from the memo pad as he gently kissed her earlobe.

"Mmmmm, you taste delicious!" he said, looking into her eyes as he returned to an upright position.

Nicole half-smiled and stepped away. "Have a good night, Mark."

She decided to return to her apartment and prepare some dinner. Perhaps she would call Mitch's number once again. She let it ring twelve times, but still no answer.

The next morning, Nicole told herself she'd give it one more try and that would be her last. It seemed like she'd tried reaching him endlessly but this time, when she finally heard him say "Hello?" she was ecstatic.

"Mitch! It's so good to hear your voice! I've been calling and calling; where have you been, Lover?" Nicole's words seemed to trip over themselves.

Mitch sounded as though he was still in bed, even though it was noon in Mapleton. "Oh, uh, Nicole! Yes, good to hear you too."

"What's going on? You sound a bit different."

"Oh, um, don't know why that is. But, listen, I'm going to have to call you back, okay? Just busy at the moment."

"Okay, that's fine; busy at what?"

"Too busy to explain just now; I'll call you when I'm free, okay?"

Nicole's voice had lost its bounce. "Yeah, sure; talk to you later." Mitch hung up the phone right away, but Nicole still held the receiver in her hand for a while before placing it back in the cradle.

She sat in silence at her kitchen table, staring into space. She'd been excited to talk to Mitch, but she didn't get the same feeling coming back across the phone lines.

Nicole took a bite of her fingernail, hoping to sort it all out when he returned her call.

VISIBLE

As morning turned into evening, and Thursday turned into Saturday, Nicole still hadn't heard from Mitch. It wasn't like him; he'd been reliable all through their relationship. Nicole fought with herself, fretting over whether to call him again or not.

This is crap! It's Saturday night in the big city, and I'm not going to be one of those girls sitting by the phone waiting for HIM to call.

Nicole pulled on her fringed, suede mini skirt and paired it with a baby blue, fitted sweater with short sleeves. To complete the look, she walked into her large closet and selected a pair of tall leather boots. Checking herself in the floor-length mirror, she was pleased with what she saw.

Heading east towards the city, her large leather handbag slung over her right shoulder, Nicole walked confidently along Robson Street, pausing to look in the windows of clothing stores along the way. When she reached the intersection of Thurlow and Robson, she saw a large sign that read *TICKETS TO ANYWHERE.*

I'm free right now; I could go anywhere. Even though she had to keep a close eye on her funds, she had made it this far. Nicole was intrigued with the mystery of what the future might hold for her.

As she passed a pet shop called Noah's Ark, she thought about owning a dog someday. Maybe a Maltese terrier. A bottle-green

MG convertible was parked on the side of the street, causing her to pause momentarily and dream about what her first car would look like. As she continued walking, she heard the side door of the gold-coloured van up ahead slide open. As she passed by, an arm darted out so fast that Nicole didn't have time to avoid the fierce grip on her left upper arm.

"Ouch! Let go of me!" she screamed with the searing pain of the assailant's pinch. Her heart pounded as she forced her right foot onto the edge of the door jamb to help resist the force trying to draw her forward into the dark cavern of the van.

Screaming for help, she twisted and turned against the strength of the dark, masked man attempting to kidnap her, and struck wildly at his head, his shoulder, anywhere where she could make contact. "Help me! Let go of me!" she yelled, trying to poke her fingers into his eyes.

Just then, the assailant cried out in agony, as her finger stabbed his left eye, forcing him to let go of her arm.

"Fuck! You Bitch!" he shouted as he pressed his left hand over his left eye and drew back into the van.

Nicole ran hard, her heart pounding in her chest, as she emitted cries of distress mixed with a sense of relief to know that she'd actually escaped. People on the street stopped to watch as she raced across the closest intersection and disappeared into a side street.

Finding a record shop open, she walked in, still breathing frantically, and tried to calm herself.

"Is there something wrong, Miss?" The young man behind the counter walked over to her. "What happened? Are you alright?"

"Yes. No. I don't know." Nicole stood by the front window, glancing left and right outside and across the street.

"Is someone following you? Do you want me to call the police?"

The few people in the store flipping through record album covers had stopped to observe this unexpected turn in their Friday night shopping experience. A slim man with dark hair walked over to the two of them and introduced himself. "Hi, I'm Officer Mosley of the Vancouver Police Department. Can you tell me what's going on?"

Nicole blurted out the story of her frightening ordeal but, the more she talked about it, the calmer she became. Officer Mosley contacted the Department with a description and location of the van, after which he continued making notes.

When he had all the information he needed, he offered to walk Nicole home.

"Thank you so much, Officer Mosley; yes, I would feel so much better if you don't mind doing that. I mean, I could take a cab..."

"It's no problem at all, Nicole; sounds like we are neighbours anyway, and I was just about to head home."

Nicole drank almost a full bottle of white wine by herself that night, not having been asked for i.d. at the liquor store by the deli. Attempting to lessen the memory of what had happened, she thought of calling her mother the next day and abruptly fell into a deep sleep.

The next morning, Nicole decided to stay in bed for a while. She got up to make some coffee then headed back under the covers, sitting up to drink, and thinking about calling Mitch. Instead, she called her mother.

Sadie picked up after the first ring. "Nicole! I've been wondering how things are going; it's already been a week since you last called."

"I know, Mum, sorry; I'm just settling in, still finding my way around town. How are you?"

"As well as you could expect, I guess. Things are pretty quiet around here since you left."

"Just think, Mom, you don't have to worry about me running around and getting pregnant anymore." Nicole regretted blurting out those words as soon as she'd heard herself say them.

The phone went uncomfortably silent. "Sorry, Mom, I shouldn't have said that. It's just that I have had a rather terrifying experience."

Nicole recounted the events of the night before, causing even more concern for Sadie.

"Nicole, maybe you should come home now. We don't have things like that happening here in Mapleton." Sadie's voice was low, her tone sad. *Could it be that my mother actually misses me?*

Nicole pictured the home she'd always lived in. Even though she'd never felt loved by her mom, and she was surrounded by cousins mercifully taken in by strangers, the familiarity of Mapleton was somehow comforting. At least she knew what to expect.

"It's not that I don't miss Mapleton, especially you and Mitch, but please understand that I need to be out on my own now that I'm done high school."

"Mitch, well, it seems like he's taken up with Holly; you know Holly, right? The girl who lives near the park?"

Nicole's heart sank; she stopped breathing, frozen in that moment. *That's why he hasn't called.* She didn't want details, the news was too painful as it stood.

"No, Mom, I didn't know that, but thanks for telling me. And I really have to go now, so thanks for the chat, and I'll try not to make it so long between calls next time."

"Okay, Nicole; good luck finding work...and please don't go walking around after dark."

"Good bye, Mom."

The news about Mitch and Holly pierced Nicole's heart. She'd only been out west for five days, and he'd taken up with someone else. And not returned her calls. *Was that all I meant to him?*

Nicole tucked her knees into her chest, pictured Mitch and

Holly side-by-side at the beach, in his beater car at night, maybe stretched out on a blanket in a farmer's field, and she began to cry, moaning out loud alone in her apartment, rocking back and forth; the bed shook as her chest heaved with grief. *This is all my fault.*

SOFT, LIKE VELVET

WITH MITCH NOW OUT OF HER LIFE, AND THREE WEEKS ON HER own without having made any meaningful connections, Nicole started to feel increasingly isolated. Despite being surrounded by the busyness of a major city, the superficial smiles and greetings imparted on the sidewalk or in shops did little to uplift her spirits and help her feel at home.

Walking along West Georgia Street on Monday morning, July 27, Nicole observed people in business attire hurrying to work, perhaps students waiting at the bus stop, others popping into shops to grab breakfast or lunch for later. Everyone seemed to have a purpose.

Nicole started to chew her nails. *Okay, I need to pull myself out of this slump and go find a job.* Her finances were running perilously low; she had started eating less, drinking less, taking the bus less, walking whenever possible.

Nicole fought numbly to regain her motivation as the week passed. She wasn't sure if the days dragged on or flew by in a state of disintegration.

Making herself read the Help Wanted ads in the Vancouver Sun, she saw lots of openings for retail sales, cashiers, and office work. Yes, she was qualified for all of those, having been one of the few of her friends who'd worked every summer plus some evenings while still in school. But Nicole longed for change.

The phone rang. She'd forgotten about Mark. "Hey, Beautiful!"

Even though he wanted to visit her at her apartment, Nicole felt unready. Too soon. Too busy.

"I get it, Nicole. Tell you what; I'll drop off a bottle of Chardonnay, give you a quick hug, and be on my way. Would that be okay?"

With Mark scheduled to arrive within the hour, Nicole did a quick clean-up. She tucked away group photographs where she'd cut a jagged circle around her head, leaving just her body; the crumply 50-dollar-bill that she planned to exchange at the bank for a new one; the sweater covered in lint and the rolls of sticky tape she intended to use to remove the unsightly fuzz.

She heard a knock on the door and went to look through the peak-hole. Mark stuck out his tongue and waggled it back and forth.

Unlatching the security chain, Nicole opened the door. Mark walked in, bottle of wine in hand, and wearing a tan leather jacket and blue-jeans. Nicole knew that she wasn't up for this scene.

"Oh, that's really sweet of you, Mark; thanks so much, and I'm sorry I can't visit today; the timing is just wrong for me right now." She smiled weakly.

"No problem, Babe." His baritone voice felt soothing to Nicole. He drew her in close and she returned the hug as Mark swept his hand under her hair and up the back of her head.

Stepping away, Nicole walked over to the living room window. "Nice view, huh? I'm pretty lucky to have gotten this apartment."

"Do you live alone, Nicole?" Mark glanced around the apartment and, entering the kitchen, asked for a glass of water.

He downed the water and walked towards the bedroom and bathroom area. "Oh, so this is where my Beauty sleeps!"

"When I can sleep."

"Oh, poor baby; I think I can help with that."

Nicole managed a small grin and then moved towards the front door. "And now, I really have to get going, Mark; maybe we could see each other next week?"

"I don't get back to the logging camp until August, so I'm hoping to see you lots before then."

By Thursday, July 30, Nicole had applied for five different jobs, none of which she actually wanted other than for practical reasons. The day was hot and sunny, and she planned to take a walk along the sea wall, maybe pop into some stores. She needed to replenish her wardrobe and prepare for possible full-time work.

Rejuvenated by the fresh sea air, Nicole felt happy to get moving again. She picked up a sandwich and headed into Eaton's department store. The upscale look with sparkling clean glass countertops, polished marble floors, and spacious elegance felt like a world apart.

On the jewelry counter, her eye was drawn to an emerald green pendant; the oval was surrounded by faux diamonds. She asked to try it on.

Fitting it around her neck, Nicole could see that the color brought out the green in her hazel eyes, and she imagined having a full strand of emerald ovals surrounded by real diamonds.

Back in her apartment, Nicole sorted her clothing purchases. She'd decided to spend $500 on work clothes, including a cream-colored wool blazer that she could wear with most of her other new items.

Feeling satisfied with her purchases, and prepared for possible employment, Nicole's self-esteem was boosted. She enjoyed a bubble bath and a glass of chilled Chardonnay before sinking into her welcoming bed.

She slipped easily into a deep sleep, so deep that the phone rang three times before she heard it, even though it was sitting on her bedside table. Half-awake, she reached for the receiver, glancing at the clock, confused. Three a.m.

"Hello?"

No response, but she could tell that the caller was still there.

Louder, she said, "Hello? Who's this?"

Still no response. She listened to the silence until the line closed. *So annoying!*

Nicole took a sip of water from the glass beside her bed, gnawed on her fingernails, rolled over, and eventually fell back to sleep.

Four a.m. Heavy breathing. This time, Nicole didn't wait until the line closed before hanging up. She could rationalize the first call, thinking it might have been a mistake. But there was no getting back to sleep after this one, so she decided to get up, have an early breakfast, and watch the sunrise.

By seven a.m. on Friday, Nicole pushed open the heavy front door of The Elaine and joined the crowds of people heading to work, school, or places unknown. She figured she fit well into the latter category. Glancing up at towering office buildings, she imagined herself dressed in a business suit, heels and designer purse, joining a group of executives in a brass-plated elevator gliding up to the 27th floor. *Maybe they need a receptionist.*

The signs of an eclectic city were everywhere: Newspaper headlines about a streaker racing across the sports field, ads for upcoming theatre productions, upcoming concerts, and Greenpeace protests. Stores selling everything from Pet Rocks to prisms, posters to crepes, window glass to hamburgers; Asian children hand-in-hand with caregivers marching across East Pender Street. Industrial cranes interspersed with buildings as the morning sun streaked across the city.

Back at The Elaine, Nicole caught sight of Colleen, the woman she'd met at her mailbox shortly after moving in. "Colleen! Hi, how's it goin'?"

"Oh hi, You; remind me of your name again?"

"It's Nicole; you can call me Nikki. Want to come up for a drink?"

As they walked down the hallway towards Nicole's apartment, they spotted what looked like a shoebox sitting on the floor directly in front of her door.

"Looks like your delivery arrived," Colleen said.

"I didn't order anything." Nicole bent down to inspect the plain cardboard box. There were no labels, no strings, or tape to secure the lid. "You know, that just seems weird," Nicole said as she removed the lid.

"Ahhhhh!" Nicole's shrill scream and abrupt movement away from the box startled Colleen, who bent down to get a better look.

"Holy shit! What the hell?"

The limp velvety body of a dead grey rat nestled in newspaper convinced Nicole that someone had it out for her. At least she knew it wasn't Colleen, judging by her reaction.

Nicole's heart thundered inside her chest. She put the lid back on and hurried down the hall and outside again where she threw the box into a garbage disposal. Colleen had followed quickly behind, and they both sat down on the bench outside, taking a moment to calm themselves.

When Nicole relayed the information about the disturbing phone calls, Colleen said, "Look, Nikki, if you ever need to flee, I'm in Apartment 106 and, here, I'll give you my number."

That night, Nicole took the receiver of her kitchen phone off the hook. When the line closed, a loud, continuous beep, beep, beep alerted her to the fact that her phone was off the hook. She covered it with a pillow, but it still didn't drown out the sound. *And what if I need to call the police in a hurry?*

Checking again and again to be sure she locked her door, Nicole dragged a kitchen chair over and wedged it under the doorknob. The phone rang. She was pretty sure it wouldn't be the dead-of-night caller at 7:30 pm.

"Mark! Oh, man, am I glad you called."

Mark listened without interrupting as she relayed the turn of events that had converted her cozy apartment into a place of fear. "Baby, sounds like you could use some lovin'. Want me to come over?"

"I would, normally, Mark, and I hope it doesn't sound like I'm always putting you off, because that's not my intention."

"If you say, Sweet Cheeks; I believe you, thousands wouldn't."

"Right now, I don't care about the thousands, I just need to tuck in tonight and restore that part of me that's had too many blows lately." Nicole paused briefly. "You know, I'll be more available for us in a few days. You understand, don't you, Mark?"

"Understood, Babe. I'll call you in a few days."

"Oh, wait! I forgot to ask you for your phone number."

"You bet! Call me anytime, especially if there are any more crazy-person incidents. I've got your back, Baby; don't you worry. My number's 604-688-8898."

Nicole felt better after talking to Mark, and now Colleen was aware as well. She thought of talking to the apartment manager in case the culprit was someone living in The Elaine. Or, she thought, it could be an outsider because, even though you needed a key to get in the front door, Nicole had seen residents hold the door open for people running up, claiming to have forgotten their key.

With her security measures in place and friends on the alert, Nicole felt a bit less uneasy going to bed that night. If the phone rang, she planned not to answer it. No satisfaction for the caller.

She looked forward to having lunch at The Naam on West Fourth with Colleen the next day.

On Saturday, August 1, as Nicole and Colleen made their way to Kitsilano, Nicole began to feel the satisfaction of finally having made some friends in Vancouver.

Exploring vegetarian cuisine for the first time, Nicole considered giving up meat. When she and Colleen got back to The Elaine it was already four pm. They'd browsed in some of the shops, walked to Kits Beach, and took a cab home.

"Would you like to come up to my place? Maybe we could order a pizza for dinner, if you want to stay," said Nicole.

"Yah, sure; I'll just pop into my apartment for a minute and then be right up. I'll bring a bottle of red."

As Nicole entered her apartment, she was overcome with the feeling that someone had been in while she was away. She didn't know why she had that feeling, and nothing seemed out of place until she walked into her bedroom closet to take off her boots.

The shocking scene before her took her breath away. She placed the palm of her hand over her mouth to quell the scream that emanated from her mouth. She walked back out from the closet, trying to remove herself from the horror of seeing her brand-new clothing slashed to pieces.

The right arm of her cream wool blazer, amputated; her pure silk blouse, cut to shreds; the skirt of her sapphire blue sheath dress, carved in the shape of a jagged circle, just like the jagged circles she'd cut in so many photographs of herself. Every piece of clothing in hangers on the rod had been lacerated in some way.

When Colleen appeared in the open doorway, she found Nicole pacing and sobbing. Nicole barely noticed Colleen's presence.

"My god! What is it, Nikki? What happened?"

All Nicole could do was motion her left arm towards the closet.

Cautiously, Colleen swung open the saloon-style doors, gasping when she saw the damage. Moving towards Nicole, Colleen wrapped her arms around her and hugged her for a long time.

"We need to call the police. And you can stay with me until it's safe again."

"I can't come back here, ever."

The police stayed for about an hour, and the clothes hangers, doors, anything that the culprit(s) could possibly have touched were dusted for fingerprints. The landlord was away, so Nicole had to wait to find out if there was another apartment available for her.

Nicole quickly gathered the few things she needed to take to Colleen's apartment that night. She now had the clothes she wore that day as well as underwear, nightclothes, and socks that remained uncut in her lingerie drawers. But the $500 she'd spent on new clothes had been wasted.

Colleen did her best to calm Nicole and to offer support as well as she could. "Don't worry, I have too many clothes anyway. Luckily, we're probably the same size, so I can easily help see you through this, Nikki."

Nicole was inconsolable. It wasn't just the loss of material things, it was the invasion of her privacy and the terror instilled in her from malicious acts aimed directly at her. *What's next? Am I going to be murdered?*

She cried herself to sleep on Colleen's fold-out couch. All she knew for sure that night was that she wanted to go home.

Waking up on the foldout, Nicole felt safe in Colleen's apartment.

Colleen had brewed a pot of coffee and stuffed some scrambled eggs into croissants.

"Today's Sunday," Colleen said, as she served Nicole her breakfast plate in bed while she herself settled into an overstuffed chair. "Let's just really take it easy today, Nikki. And you can stay here, safe with me, until there's a vacancy somewhere else."

Almost whispering, Nicole felt depleted. "Thank you for being such a good friend, Colleen."

"I'm going to see you through this, Nikki; you're not alone."

The next morning, Nicole lay in bed while Colleen got ready for work.

Are you going to be okay staying here by yourself today?" Colleen asked.

Nicole had slept soundly. "Yes, I'll be okay. And if I may borrow some clothes, I'll probably go shopping for a few things."

"Help yourself to whatever you need, Nikki, honestly. And how 'bout we meet back here at four-thirty. Maybe we can take a walk in Stanley Park then get some take-out for dinner."

"Yes, I'd love that, Colleen, thanks. See you at four-thirty."

After Colleen left, Nicole sat by the window in the sun and dialed Mark's number. "Wrong number" said a female voice on the other end of the line.

I must have written it down wrong.

Nicole longed for the warmth of Mark's arms, his tender caress, and his upbeat personality. He'd be a good distraction from the horror of the night before. But she'd have to wait for him to call; then, she remembered that the phone number he had was for the phone in Apartment 304. How they could possibly connect, she didn't know. Nicole let out a heavy sigh.

Locating the box where she'd put her bank information, she sat down at the kitchen table to check her bank balance. Disheartened to see that it was just under $2000, she knew she no longer had the luxury of spending $500 on new clothes.

Dressed in one of Colleen's summer dresses, Nicole looked both ways before stepping out into the hallway.

The stores weren't busy on a Monday morning, and Nicole was pleased to find a few inexpensive items of clothing that would tide her over for the first few weeks of a new job.

She picked up a ham sandwich for a late lunch on her way to the seawall, planning to relax and enjoy the sunshine until it was time to meet Colleen at four-thirty.

After a leisurely walk, taking time to stop and appreciate the beauty surrounding the city, Nicole found a spot to sit on a grassy hill overlooking the water.

The sky was a mix of cloud and sun by then, so Nicole didn't feel the need for shade. She unwrapped her sandwich and ravenously took a bite. The fresh sea air and exercise had made her extra hungry. She finished the sandwich in record time, crumpled the waxed paper wrap, and placed it in her paper bag. Enjoying the ambiance, unrestricted by commitments other than her dinner date with Colleen, Nicole soaked in the gorgeous afternoon. Her commitment to staying in Vancouver re-emerged in those moments. She focussed on the freighters out on the strait, and the people passing by. In her peripheral vision, she noticed a figure moving up the hill in her direction.

A tall, handsome man dressed in a long-collared, sky-blue shirt and off-white dress pants gave her a warm smile as he greeted her.

"Hi! You looked so relaxed up here, I thought I might join you if that's okay."

Judging by his salt-and-pepper hair, Nicole guessed that he was in his late forties. His black oxfords looked like they'd been freshly shined, but the first few buttons of his shirt were left open and he wasn't wearing a tie.

"Oh! Sure, you're welcome to join me, but you might want to think about grass stains on those light slacks." Nicole smiled, looking into his gorgeous turquoise eyes.

"I know; I'm just a carefree kind of guy, I guess." And he sat next to her, turning towards Nicole and extending his right hand. "I'm Jared Sinclair." He looked directly into Nicole's eyes, causing her stomach to thrill. *He's probably old enough to be my father.*

After Nicole introduced herself and they shook hands, Jared began a conversation that lasted an hour; much too short, as far as Nicole was concerned.

"Isn't this a great place to sit and watch the world go by, Nicole?"

"I love it. This is so different from the world I grew up in..." and they chatted about their individual lives, with Jared seeming to be keenly interested in the fact that Nicole was looking for work.

"What skills do you have?" The look of amusement in Jared's eyes didn't go unnoticed by Nicole.

"Well, I just graduated in June; Ontario Grade 13. But I've worked from the time I was 15 while still in school, and then every summer in a life insurance company as a secretary."

"Good for you, Nicole. I admire your ambition. So many young people today seem to have little drive."

"I can tell you that most of the students in my graduating class had no idea of where they wanted to go, other than to take the year off and travel."

"And what do you want to do?" asked Jared.

"Ha! Well, I won't pretend to be much different. I just knew that I had to get out of my hometown and live my own life. I figured that a city as big as Vancouver could accommodate me and my need to find a job."

Nicole paused for a moment. "And, to tell you the truth, I want to make a lot of money. I'm not shy about saying that, either. I've seen too many families struggle to try and make ends meet."

Jared's interest was apparent as his eyes seemed to sharpen. "So, do you just want to make ends meet, or do you aspire to loftier goals, Nicole?"

"Loftier. I want to have enough money that I don't have to think twice about buying an emerald necklace, if you know what I mean." Nicole might not have been so blatant if she'd actually known this guy. In a foreign city, talking to a stranger, she felt comfortable just speaking her mind.

"A city or town of any size would, I'm sure, be willing to accommodate a young woman as beautiful as you." Jared smiled, moving his eyes down the length of her body, making Nicole feel a little uncomfortable while, at the same time, allowing herself to be flattered. *Come on; for real? I can't seriously be attracted to this guy.*

Jared reached over and picked up Nicole's left hand. "My aunt was a palm reader, and I learned a few things from her...if I may?"

Nicole held her breath as the sensations she felt in her palm seemed to reach deep down into her soul as he gently traced her lines with his fingertip.

"You have a long life ahead, but I see that there's been some trauma along the way. And, oh, this is interesting. Your love life is about to take a sensational turn, one that will leave you reeling."

Jared's eyes were soft, gently smiling, as he looked at Nicole.

She could barely keep her composure. So entranced was she with Jared's touch and the sound of his voice, that she barely noticed Mark pass close by, close enough that he couldn't have missed her.

"And I may have some news of interest to you, Nicole, regarding a job opening at the Hillside campus of Everton College. If you'd like to hear more about it, I'd be happy to take you out for dinner tomorrow night and let you know the details."

Nicole was extra hungry these days, desperate for work, albeit the right kind of work, and still missing Mitch.

"Jared, thank you; I'd be delighted to accept your kind invitation."

They rose from the ground, sweeping bits of debris from their clothing. "It's a date, then," Jared chuckled, seeming pleased with himself. "I'll pick you up at seven p.m. tomorrow. Do you like seafood?"

"I do, the few times I've had it. It's not so popular where I'm from. But I've heard that west coast seafood is the best, so I'm excited to try it."

"Sounds perfect, then, Nicole. Just bring your appetite and your lovely smile, and I'll make a reservation at The Sea Breeze. See you at seven."

As Jared walked away and disappeared into the distance, Nicole reflected on what had just happened. *This is either my lucky day, my meant-to-be, or a horrible, stupid move on my part, something I may regret forever.*

Still only 18 years of age, Nicole was open-minded and positive-thinking, despite having gotten off to a bad start in Vancouver. *I didn't even ask him what the job entailed, but he seemed to want me to wait until tomorrow evening.* She weighed the possible outcomes, as she saw them. *If I get a job out of this, make a new friend, and am able to continue living in my apartment, then it'll be well worth it. If it doesn't work out, I will at least be fed.*

It was already four o'clock when Nicole got back to The Elaine and found Mark sitting on the bench, a brown paper bag by his side.

"Woah! What a surprise, Mark," and she walked over to greet him with a hug. "You know, I tried calling you this morning, but it was the wrong number."

"Uh-huh, well that's too bad because I tried calling you too, but no answer at all." He shrugged his shoulders and looked at her, waiting for her reply.

Nicole sat down and told him about the break-in, her slashed clothing, and her temporary accommodation with Colleen. "Nikki, you didn't deserve that! Have you been back to the apartment since?"

"No." Nicole looked down. "It's the last place I want to go right now, even though I still need to get a few things from there."

"Well, I'm here for you, Babe; I told you, I have your back. Let's go up there right now, and I'll help you carry away what you need."

"Aw, thanks, Mark; you know, that's not a bad idea if you don't mind just waiting a moment while I set down my parcels. Then, I'll come back and get you."

"I'll be here, Sweet Cheeks," he said, winking at her and sitting back down on the bench.

Setting down her parcels, Nicole grabbed a pen and paper and scribbled a note to Colleen. "I'm just in Apartment 304 for a moment; don't worry, Mark's with me. Come up and help us carry down a few things?"

Nicole unlocked the door of her apartment then stood aside while Mark turned the knob and swung it open. Then he stepped aside, making a sweeping motion with his hand.

"After you, Beautiful."

He shut the door rather forcefully, Nicole thought, and then, in an instant, he'd taken a roll of duct tape from his paper bag, unrolled a long strip and, with lightning speed, covered her mouth, wrapping it around the back of her head twice.

Traumatized, Nicole tried to scream behind the tape as he reefed her arms around behind her and bound her wrists. Walking into the bathroom, he found a towel. As he draped the towel over the top of her head, she could hear the sound of another strip of tape being unrolled from the spool. He wound another strip around the towel also at the level of her mouth. At least she could still breathe behind the terrycloth, and maybe, in some way, it was better that she could no longer look at the monster as he assaulted her.

Nicole felt sick, trying hard not to vomit when her mouth was obstructed with tape. Behind the towel, her eyes were wide with terror as she tried to make herself calm down.

"Oofff!" Nicole cried out in agony as her body was thrown onto the hard floor, her left shoulder taking the brunt of the force. He rolled her over onto her back.

Her awareness of shoulder pain was supplanted by terror as he pushed her skirt up toward the top of her hips, and she felt the sharp pinch of his fingernails as he groped for her underpants.

Just then, the apartment door swung open. Colleen gasped in horror as she instinctively backed into the hallway, screaming at the top of her lungs. "Help! Help us! Help! Help!"

Mark lurched towards Colleen as people poured out into the hallway, hurrying towards the scene. Mark raced into the hallway, attempting to escape. Swiftly, he was tackled to the ground by some quick-thinking men, and Colleen rushed back into the apartment to free her friend and call the police.

Utterly shaken by the assault, Nicole was grateful for Colleen's support. She did her best to thank everyone who rushed to her aid, but could hardly hold back tears as Colleen helped her navigate the hallways and stairs back to Colleen's apartment.

Her heart was still racing as she drank the glass of water offered by Colleen. It felt good to be back in Colleen's apartment, two floors away from the scene of the crime. But if only she could get the pictures out of her mind. The abrupt turn from friend to enemy, the sudden obscurity behind the towel, the panicked fright of being silenced by duct tape, the pain of being shoved to the hard floor, and the dreaded fear when he slid her skirt up over her hips. She reviewed each event as if watching a movie where the same scene kept playing over and over again.

"Let me help you get that duct tape out of your hair." In the bathroom, Colleen patiently used the heat of her hair blower, set on low, to help loosen the top edge of the tape. She worked patiently and slowly as the glue started to melt, enabling her eventually to remove the tape.

"What would I do without you, Colleen?"

Colleen brushed her fingers over the sticky residue left on the back of Nicole's hair. "Not quite finished just yet. Give me a minute and I'll go get some oil from the kitchen."

Colleen returned with a small bowl of vegetable oil. Dipping her fingers into the bowl, she massaged the oil into Nicole's hair strands from the stickiness all the way down to the tips. Then, using a comb and applying more oil as needed, Colleen was able to loosen the matted hair and eventually free the strands.

Nicole turned around and hugged Colleen. "Thank you, dear friend." She held Colleen for longer than usual, wanting her to know how grateful she was, and then she said, "I can't wait to have a shower and wash off any trace of that monster."

"Maybe that calls for some bleach," Colleen joked as she headed towards the kitchen. "I'll figure out something for us to eat." Colleen tried to lighten things up, despite feeling quite shaken herself.

As Nicole stepped into the shower, she had to keep reminding herself that she was now safe. But she couldn't get the frightening scenes out of her head. The horror of what did happen and the thought of what might have happened caused her to vomit. Her chest heaved as she tried to suppress her grief so Colleen wouldn't hear, but torrents of salty tears streamed down her face and into her mouth.

She tilted her head back and opened her mouth, letting the soothing hot water wash away evidence of her distress and her shame. *How could you be so stupid?*

Stepping out of the shower, Nicole wrapped herself in a bath towel and used a smaller towel to dry her hair. She'd chosen a pair of pajamas over a nighty, wanting to feel more clothed. By the time she walked back into the living room and her fold-out bed, she felt exhausted.

"Nikki, would you like to sleep in my room tonight? I can sleep out here."

Nicole hung her head and thought for a moment. "You know, I'd like that, Colleen. I don't want to put you out but, in all honesty, I just need to go in there, close the door, and shut out the world."

She climbed into bed at six-thirty, pulling the covers high up under her chin. Colleen entered the room and placed her favorite wool blanket on top of the covers to add some extra weight and warmth.

Looking at Nicole's pale face, she asked, "Are you sure you don't want anything to eat?"

"I can't even think about food right now." Nicole closed her eyes.

"How 'bout some soft music to help you drift off to sleep?"

Without responding, Nicole closed her eyes. Colleen found a classical music station, turned the volume down, turned out the lights, and gently closed the bedroom door as she left the room.

As much as Nicole's tired body begged her to sleep, her racing mind wouldn't allow it. Rolling left, then right, sitting up to sip some water, turning on the light to read, nothing worked.

Eventually falling asleep around three a.m., Nicole woke with a start when she heard the duct tape unrolling, felt it tighten around her mouth, corralling her hair as it circled around the back of her head, muffling her screams of terror. *Did darkness exacerbate the fear of the unknown, the helplessness of being bound and gagged?*

She was restless from then until she heard Colleen getting ready for work. But Nicole made herself stay in bed until after Colleen left, not wanting to talk about the attack.

When she finally got up and opened the bedroom door, she could see that the morning was incongruously filled with sunshine. Like in the aftermath of losing a loved one, Nicole wanted it to be a dull day because sunshine didn't fit the loss that she so keenly felt the morning after the attack.

Trying to make the morning seem normal, she thought about coffee but felt nauseous as soon as she imagined the smell. She managed a piece of toast with scant butter and a warm glass of milk. Barely.

Forcing herself to get dressed in a cozy sweatsuit, and not wearing any makeup, she opened the door of Colleen's apartment and peered out into the hallway. Up and down. No people, no action. Reaching the foyer, she walked right by a man checking his mailbox, jumping as he slammed the mailbox door shut. The coldness of metal against metal sent a chill down Nicole's spine.

"Hey! Aren't you the woman who was attacked yesterday?"

Nicole glanced over her shoulder as she opened the heavy front door of the building, "I have to go now," is all she could manage. She let the door close as she walked away from The Elaine, hoping for solitude in Stanley Park.

Hours passed by as Nicole sat on a bench, oblivious to her surroundings. Anger arose as she thought of how Mark had fooled her. How she'd allowed herself to be fooled by Mark. So that it was her fault, not Mark's. She'd dressed to attract, she'd led him on. She wasn't there when he'd expected her to be. And then he'd seen her with Jared. *What did I think would happen?*

Questions without answers and confusing thoughts began to torment Nicole the longer she sat on the park bench, creating chaos in her mind. *How could anyone treat another human being that way?* Followed by, *It's not really that big of a deal, is it? I mean, he didn't rape me. He didn't actually rape me...but he was about to. If it wasn't for Colleen, he would have raped me.*

GO AHEAD WITHOUT ME

SCATTERED WAVES OF PACIFIC BLUE SPARKLED UNDER THE WARM sunshine on the 25th of August, a seascape completely lost on Nicole. The fresh sea air usually made her feel rejuvenated. As a tall stranger approached the vicinity of her bench, Nicole could feel her muscles tense. Peaking sideways over the edge of her hood, she observed a male jogger, who smiled as he passed by. Nicole drew back, busying herself by rummaging through her handbag.

Although it at first appeared to be a safe place to sit and try to sort through what had happened to her, Nicole now felt it unsafe even in this wide-open environment. She drew her knees up to her chest, trying not to feel overwhelmed with her own thoughts.

Perhaps she should go back to the apartment. Would she feel safer in that enclosed environment with nothing but her own thoughts to occupy her? Or should she wait until Colleen got home so she'd have someone to talk to? But did she actually want to talk about it? Is it better to be alone or with lots of people?

Nicole couldn't decide what to do and sat there still, feeling overwhelmed and vulnerable.

"You don't happen to have a wrench, do you, Miss?"

A young man wearing shorts and a tee-shirt had stopped close to Nicole's bench and kneeled beside his bicycle. She unavoidably glanced up, half-smiling at his absurd question, figuring he was looking to connect with her. She stood up from the bench and headed back towards the apartment, her decision made.

As Nicole unlocked the door of Apartment 103, she was greeted by the smell of fried onions. Colleen, who was just leaving the bathroom, seemed happy to see Nicole, probably glad that she'd ventured outside the apartment.

"Nikki! How're you doing today, Sweetness?"

Nicole smiled shortly, unzipping her hoodie. "Oh, I'm fine, thanks, Colleen; how 'bout you?"

"Good! I thought about you all day; I called, but no answer. I'm so glad you're feeling better, but I must say that you look a little pale."

"Oh, probably because I didn't bother to put on my makeup today. I mean, what's the point? I'm not trying to attract anyone." And they both chuckled.

Nicole grew serious, her brow furrowed. "Speaking of the phone, you know, I completely forgot that I had a dinner invitation for tonight...the last thing I feel like doing ...but I don't want to be rude, either." Fretting, she wrung her hands together, and said, "I don't know what to do."

"Don't worry, Nikki; I'll take care of it." When Colleen went to call Jared, she played a message on her answering machine first. Jared's voice said that he'd pick Nicole up at seven, and he left his number in case that didn't work for her.

"Ohmygod! That's only 2 1/2 hours from now, Colleen. What am I going to do?"

"It's okay, Nikki; please try to calm down." Colleen motioned towards the sofa, hoping Nicole would relax while she returned the call.

"Hello, Jared; I'm Nikki's roommate Colleen. She's really under the weather tonight, so she's going to stay in. But she asked me to thank you for your kindness, and she sends her regrets."

"Oh, I'm sorry to hear that, Colleen. Please tell her I hope she's well soon. Perhaps we can reconnect next week, then?"

"Possibly. I'll give her the message, Jared. You have a good evening."

Nicole felt relieved that there was one less thing to deal with.

Over the next four weeks, Nicole struggled to ground herself. Upon Colleen's recommendation, she underwent regular sessions with a counselor who specialized in female assault issues. At first, she giggled nervously, while relating the events leading up to the attack. As the counselor listened attentively, Nicole began to wail as she relayed the specifics of the surprise attack in her own apartment, a place where she'd felt safe, and a place that she'd envisioned as the launchpad to her new life out west.

"How did that make you feel, Nicole, when he hooked his fingers under the rim of your underwear?"

Nicole began to cry uncontrollably as she relived the attack in front of someone other than Colleen. She made good use of the tissue box nearby and, when that session ended for the day, Nicole experienced a feeling of calmness for the first time in weeks.

She found a chiropractor who specialized in shoulder injuries and soon found that she experienced less pain in her left shoulder where it had crashed into the hard surface of the living room floor that day. The range of motion in her rotator cuff was slowly restored, and she performed specific exercises to help reinforce all the good that had been done.

Self-care felt especially good following the violence aimed directly at Nicole. The caring hands of her female massage therapist were the only ones she would allow to touch her body now.

EMERGING

By week four following the incident, Nicole had just begun to feel a bit more like herself. She'd been awakened many nights with a recurrent nightmare where she was chased by a blurry figure in the dark. Racing as fast as she could, her heart hammering against her chest, Nicole felt her right foot sink into a gopher hole. Grappling with the agony of a twisted ankle, and the figure fast-approaching, she woke up just before his pointed, bony fingers could reach her.

The nightmare was terrifying, no matter how many times it ran through her head. Each time, she shook with fear the closer the figure came, and as the inevitable was about to happen. She'd awaken, breathing hard, a layer of sweat enveloping her body. She'd rub her ankle, even though it was fine.

Colleen hadn't heard any sounds coming from the fold-out where Nicole slept, so Nicole figured her screams had somehow been muffled.

While her self-care treatments were necessary and effective, she hadn't budgeted for those expenses. Nicole had to find work or she'd have to go back home, and in the deepest part of her soul, she knew she couldn't allow that to happen. To return home, humiliated and defeated, was not on Nicole's agenda.

Colleen had left for work and Nicole had some time to kill before her job interview at 10:00. An architect's office on West Georgia was looking for a receptionist.

On a small table just inside the front door of Colleen's apartment, Nicole noticed a stack of paper currency. Leafing through, she saw that there were four twenties, two tens, three fives, five twos, and five ones. One hundred and thirty dollars.

And Nicole was short. She wondered if she'd have enough money for her share of the groceries that week, and twenty dollars would likely make up what was needed.

Picking up the stack of paper money, she carefully thumbed through the twenties to be sure that there were four. She removed one, walked over to her purse on the kitchen table, and stuffed it into her wallet. *Colleen won't miss it. She'll probably think she miscounted.*

While browsing through the bookshelf in the waiting room of the architect's office, Nicole began flipping through the pages of an art book. There, she was mesmerized by the replication of an artwork by Hans Memling, a 15th-century artist, entitled Allegory of Chastity.

Nicole stared at the mysterious painting, which depicted a young woman standing in the middle of a giant piece of amethyst spears. She read the accompanying notes and found that the woman's virginity was represented by her crossed hands placed in her lap and on one point of the crystal as she gazed downward. Nicole was amused, remembering her mother's directive, when it came to the male gender, "Keep your legs crossed, Nicole." The color of the amethyst represented the violet flower, which symbolized humility and virginity.

Two lions carrying golden shields protected the stream, whose current brought forth gemstones representing Paradise. The spring itself represented the Water of Life.

I like the idea of a woman's precious virginity being protected.

The notes continued, associating the strength of Virginity with eternal life.

Nicole's eye was drawn to a book about famous sculptures. She was captivated by a 19th century marble sculpture by Auguste Rodin called *The All-Devouring Female*. She read the description, written by the artist himself. "The woman dominates and forcibly exhausts the man whom she has leapt upon as if a prey, and he does not resist."

A woman using force to exhaust her sexual partner? Nicole was intrigued.

"Excuse me, Nicole; Mr. Rauche will see you now."

Nicole had prepared herself for the handshake, role-playing how she would raise the thumb of her right hand and place the joint over his thumb joint, then curve her fingers around and wrap the back of his hand. Nothing she hadn't done before. But this would be the first time she touched a man since the attack.

Here he comes. Smile, raise thumb, swoop in for the shake, two pumps then back off.

When Nicole opened the door of Colleen's apartment, Colleen's first words were, "Did you get the job?"

"It's mine if I want it." Nicole said matter-of-factly.

"Sounds like you're not exactly passionate about being a receptionist for an architectural firm."

"It has its advantages, Colleen, but I can't say that it's my dream job, that's for sure."

"D'you have any more interviews set up for tomorrow?"

"No. But I think I'll spend some time at the library."

Nicole selected as many books as she could carry about bondage, a world completely unknown to her other than the news of Rodin's sculpture yesterday morning. The more she read, and the more pictures she looked at, the more intrigued she became.

I was bound and gagged with duct tape. In a different circumstance, that could look like a game leading to sexual arousal.

As she delved into the practice of BDSM, the idea of *tease and denial* appealed to her. She'd apparently been good at teasing, but not been given the opportunity to deny. Yet.

What piqued her interest most of all was an intense form of power-play called "resistance play". Nicole's mind latched on to the idea of her assaulting Jared, taking his power away before he could take away hers. *Make him be the submissive, force him to do something against his will.* Nicole was fascinated.

When Nicole returned to the apartment, Colleen was not home yet. She slouched down on the sofa in the quiet surroundings and thought about what she had learned.

Am I really going from being assaulted to learning how to be the assaulter myself? The idea reminded her of a 'Kill or be killed' philosophy. *Maybe if I learn how to do this, I'll be less vulnerable to non-consensual sex.*

But things weren't that simple. Nicole battled with herself over questions such as *Will I ever be able to have a normal sex life again? Do I even care? Is it a woman's destiny to give herself over to a man? Will I be safe? Can I trust my partner to play by the rules?*

Once again, Nicole began to feel overwhelmed with so many questions. But who could she trust to help her get through her sexual predicament? Maybe the mysterious painting depicting chastity was more on point. *But that is not who I am.*

Colleen arrived home to find Nicole looking unsettled. "Something wrong, Nicole?"

"No, everything's fine."

Colleen came and sat beside Nicole on the sofa. "You know, I hope you don't blame yourself for any of this. No one deserves to be sexually assaulted."

"They sure don't," Nicole said, while thinking about her tentative plan to assault Jared.

"I feel as though I have a label on my back now. It says, "Assault Victim". I mean, is there a special line-up I need to get into to help identify myself?"

"Of course not, Nicole, and I can see how you might think of yourself as being singled out."

"Here's the thing, Colleen; you don't have a clue what this feels like, and I hope you never do." Nicole didn't mean to raise her voice.

"You're right, I don't. But I do know what it feels like to be different. My dad is an albino black, my mom is from the Philippines. Kids used to tease me at school, saying things like, 'Why are you acting black, when you're not black? You don't even look Phillipino. You're not black, you're not white. What are you, anyway?'

Colleen found Nicole's bad mood to be uninviting. As she stood up from the sofa, her hand swung into a drinking glass and smashed it to the floor. Nicole jumped and screamed, then she started to shake.

Colleen found a warm blanket and placed it around Nicole. "It's okay, Colleen; I'll leave you in peace while I go make dinner."

Colleen cleaned up the breakage and then left Nicole to settle herself. As she walked into the kitchen, Colleen gently advised Nicole to "try and think of things that make you smile."

When Colleen wasn't looking, Nicole replaced the twenty-dollar bill she'd stollen from Colleen's stack at the front entrance.

What's happening to me? If I can't trust even myself, then who can I trust?

❖

That night in bed, Nicole continued to read up on her new interest, in preparation for tomorrow's dinner date with Jared.

The Dominatrix was a fascinating read for Nicole. To her, the idea of hurting her partner during sexual activity in order to give him pleasure sounded foreign and just plain wrong. And giving him humiliating tasks to do, such as licking her boots, sounded more childish than adult to Nicole.

But the idea of wearing a thick, impenetrable cat suit that revealed her feminine shapes appealed to Nicole as much as the chaste woman standing in the middle of an amethyst. *Tease and denial* was a new phrase for Nicole, but she was catching on fast.

Nonetheless, Nicole couldn't hide her interest and excitement over the idea of forcing the submissive to do something against his will, an intense form of power play.

It's all about power, isn't it? Maybe life was a game that she hadn't played very well, so far. But things were about to change.

RENDEZVOUS

FROM COLLEEN'S LIVING ROOM WINDOW, NICOLE HAD SEEN JARED pull up in a shiny red mustang convertible. Top-down. White leather seats. She hurried down the stairs towards the front door, taking a moment to compose herself before Jared would see her.

"Hello!" Jared got out and came around to the passenger side, opening the car door for Nicole. She had fitted on three different outfits that evening, two belonging to Colleen, uncertain of what to wear. Judging by his attire that afternoon in the park, Nicole had settled on a slim and sleek black cocktail dress, with a below-the-knee-length hem and a boat neck that highlighted her youthful bone structure and enhanced her long, slender neck. The three-quarter-length sleeves showed off her slim arms and long-fingered hands. She chose her four-inch heels to complement Jared's tall frame. *At least Mark didn't slash my shoes.*

The Sea Breeze Restaurant sat high on a hill overlooking English Bay. The nautical décor was intriguing to Nicole, who'd never seen the ocean before moving west. Large green glass fisherman's balls mingled with displays of starfish, conch shells, clam shells, and seashells she couldn't identify surrounded a giant piece of coral displayed on a round table in the entranceway to the restaurant. The oceanside windows were enormous, and set in a semi-circular fashion to take advantage of the 180-degree view.

"Oh, this place is gorgeous, Jared! And I can't wait to try their seafood."

"Tell you what, Nicole; how about I order for you?"

"Okay, you're the expert, Jared." Nicole enjoyed all the attention and special treatment, but she had learned the hard way not to trust a stranger. Yet, this was only dinner.

Two glasses of ice water were set down on the white linen tablecloth, and the waiter asked if they'd like to order other drinks. "I'm going to order a martini, Nicole, and maybe we could enjoy our drinks on the verandah; would you like that?"

Nicole smiled, knowing that the legal age for drinking was 19, making her underaged by 7 months. Turning to the waiter, Jared ordered a gin martini, and Nicole ordered a Tom Collins, focussing on sounding confident as if ordering alcoholic beverages was something she did all the time. The waiter said he'd bring them out to the verandah.

The warm summer evening started to cool as a gentle breeze came up. Sunlight streamed across the water, and the edges of the small waves caught the light, creating a satiny glimmer across the sea. Nicole felt as if she were on vacation. They were the only two on the verandah, although the restaurant was close to full capacity.

The waiter arrived with their drinks on a round tray. When he left, Jared and Nicole toasted to "warm summer evenings just like this." Boat traffic was light, with just a few pleasure boats tucked in for the night, their lights warning others of their position on the water. The long, sandy beach looked inviting, and Nicole hoped to return sometime during daylight hours.

Resting his arms on the railing while leaning forward and gazing out to sea, Jared said, "There's going to be a beautiful sunset tonight," as the sun lowered closer to the sea like a big, fiery, blood-orange ball of radiance, sending streamers of gold, orange, and pink across the evening sky. Sinking deep into the horizon, the sun created a wide path which shimmered across the bay towards Nicole and Jared, like a welcome mat to another world.

Just then, a gentle breeze blew a strand of Nicole's hair into her face, and Jared leaned towards her, sweeping it away with his thumb.

Nicole jumped, instinctively drawing back, then smiled awkwardly. *That's rather forward! Maybe I need to stick a pin into that over-inflated ego of his.*

"Oh, I'm sorry, Nicole; I didn't mean to startle you. Shall we go back to our table?" Jared asked, as he motioned Nicole to go ahead of him.

Soft jazz played in the background as they took their places. The small hurricane lamp in the center of the table had been lit. Nicole was a romantic at heart, and tonight's setting reminded her of tender moments spent with Mitch.

When the waiter returned, Jared ordered cracked Dungeness crab with warm lemon garlic butter.

"Nicole, you're in for a treat."

"Well, it sounds wonderful; thanks for ordering for me. No one's ever done that before."

Jared smiled, more to himself than to Nicole. "Here's to many more firsts for you, my dear." And he raised his glass in a toast to Nicole. "Now, I'm sure you're anxious to hear about the opportunity I may have for you."

Nicole interlaced her fingers, placed her elbows on the table, and rested her chin on her interlaced fingers as if to better focus her attention on what Jared was about to say.

"There is a teaching vacancy in the Business Office Training Division at Hillside College. This would involve teaching Typing and Office Procedures, as a starting point, with lots of opportunity to advance over time, provided we are satisfied with your work." Jared nodded his head slightly.

"But I have no experience teaching." Nicole began to feel disappointed, figuring that her inexperience and lack of training would rule her out immediately.

"You have practical experience in an office setting, and at Everton we regard that as more important than teacher training and teaching experience."

"Really? I would have thought that teachers had to be trained how to teach."

"Not at the community college level, no. "

"What if I wasn't any good at teaching; I mean..." Nicole's concern was evidenced in a slight frown and staring eyes as if she were picturing herself at the front of a class that paid her no heed and were instead chatting amongst themselves, getting out of their desks at will, and generally disrespecting her. She tried not to bite her nails.

"You don't have to worry, Nicole. I can easily see that you are a smart woman, you're well-spoken, you present well. Anything you need, we can show you and, if all goes well, you'll probably be heading the program yourself one day."

Why does he seem to want me there so badly?

"Well, I sure appreciate your letting me know about the vacancy, Jared and, yes, I'd be very interested in applying."

Jared looked pleased, his turquoise eyes tender and smiling in the glow of the candlelight.

"How do I apply, then?"

"Consider this your application, for now, Nicole. I'll handle the rest, starting with introducing you to Kendra Howard. She's the coordinator of the program, and we three will be working closely together, so I want to make sure you're a good match."

"All right. When would you like me to meet her...is it "Mrs. Howard?""

"Her office will give you a call and set up the appointment. And, yes, it's Mrs. Howard, but I'm sure she'll want you to call her Kendra."

As though noticing the look of concern on Nicole's face, Jared said, "Look. Just leave it with me, and things will be clearer as time goes on. The only thing you have to do for now is to impress Kendra."

"Any tips on how to impress Kendra?" Nicole was getting sleepy, but tried to remain focussed.

"Yes, dress especially well and just be your impressive self."

Just then, two steaming plates of cracked crab were served, along with lemon garlic butter dipping sauce placed in a stainless-steel warming pot. Roasted asparagus, bell peppers, onions, and broccoli accompanied the crab, along with lemon rice pilaf.

"A bottle of Chardonnay, please," Jared ordered without asking Nicole if she liked Chardonnay.

In the courtyard of The Sea Breeze, Jared opened the car door for Nicole. She stepped out onto the pavement, preparing to express her appreciation for such a wonderful dinner and the opportunity of a job. Before she could say anything, Jared interjected. "You know, if you don't have any other plans at the moment, I'd like to explain a few more important aspects of this position to you."

Through the haze of the evening's events, and considering the month-ago trauma that was still fresh in her mind, Nicole hesitated.

Is this going to lead to another assault? I don't even know this guy.

Nicole became leery of Jared's motives for wanting to extend their visit, which to her seemed quite complete already. As she thought about how things had gone, from meeting Jared on a grassy knoll overlooking the water, to the magic of this evening, she wondered how things could get any stranger, any more wonderful. She was aware that the cocktail and glasses of Chardonnay may have helped influence her thinking.

Jared interjected, "I rent an apartment nearby; I think you'll like it."

Jared stood before her, awaiting her response, and looking even more handsome when the moonlight caught his strands of silvery hair.

He'd been courteous, although not entirely respectful, Nicole reasoned. She'd done some sleuthing before meeting Jared for the second time. She'd called Everton College and asked to speak to Jared Sinclair, then hung up when she heard his voice on the other end of the line. *He's not Mark.*

She thought about how much she needed a job, knowing that her staying in Vancouver depended on it. And this wasn't any job; it was a job that could elevate her to greater things, things she'd longed for. Things that could legitimize her departure from Mapleton, Ontario, and not make her look like a laughingstock. *Don't blow it.*

But the new Nicole had other plans. As Jared searched for his keys, she pretended to help.

"I'll go back and ask at the front desk if anyone turned them in," and off she went.

Jared checked under the seat with a flashlight, between the seats, and on the pavement underneath the car.

As Jared headed back to check the men's room, Nicole was coming outside again. She was good at concealing her pleasure in having confiscated and disposed of his keys when he'd left the dinner table to use the men's room.

Tease had been successfully orchestrated, but there was a second opportunity for Nicole to get more practice at this game.

"It's no big deal; people lose their keys all the time," said Jared.

To Nicole, Jared's comment seemed a little too dismissive, considering how easily the keys were lost over a very limited area.

"Look, I'll call a cab, and we can carry on as planned," he strategized.

Nicole placed her hand on Jared's shoulder and said, "I'm so sorry, Jared, I'm going to have to give it a miss. I'm just not feeling well; I need to go home."

"Oh, well, okay, Nicole; I hope it wasn't the cracked crab."

They went their separate ways, and Nicole was left to take off her sexy evening clothes and sink into a hot bath. *I hope I'm not falling into a world where I don't belong.*

Nicole had accepted a second invitation to Jared's apartment, the following Saturday, October 3rd, and she looked at this as an opportunity to practise her craft.

Jared served Bailey's on ice in crystal brandy snifters as they stood soaking in the view of city lights from the balcony of his penthouse apartment on Broadway.

"Are you married, Jared?"

"Yes." He nodded decisively without looking at Nicole.

"Why do I think there's a 'but' attached to that 'Yes'?"

Jared grinned like a little boy. "Let me put it this way. When you've been married to the same woman for twenty years, well...." And he didn't finish his sentence.

"Okay." Nicole felt awkward, and decided to change the subject. "Now, what else did you have to tell me about the teaching position, Jared?"

Jared turned his body towards Nicole and set his brandy snifter down on a cocktail table. "Well, you know Nicole, I needed a reason to spend a few more hours with you," and he moved in closer.

Nicole stood still, quietly looking at Jared in cautious anticipation, while feeling the dulling effects of alcohol. When he placed his hands on her waist, leaned down, and gently brushed his lips against hers with exquisite delicacy, Nicole felt as though she was only half there.

When he led her into the bedroom, softly lit by the bedside table lamps, Nicole halted. "Jared, stop!" she ordered.

Jared turned to look at her, a mix of puzzlement and surprise on his face.

Nicole placed her hands at the top of the button panel on his shirt, and tugged it downward, with just enough force to cause a half-smile on Jared's lips. Keeping her expression solemn, she quickly released one button after another, exposing Jared's bare chest. The image in Nicole's mind was much more forceful, with her tearing open his shirt, buttons falling in all directions, but this was a start.

Nicole could feel Jared's intrigue as he stood there, watching steadily as she took the lead. Looking down, Nicole slid the backs of her fingers against his belly and behind the waist band of his pants. She stayed there for a moment, raising her head to look up at Jared, still with a straight face, and holding his gaze for a few seconds that felt more like minutes to her. Fighting her urge to go too quickly, to make her statement and then get out, Nicole forced herself to slow down.

Removing her fingers from behind his waist band, she then grabbed onto his belt buckle, yanking it towards her before undoing the buckle itself, giving her access to the button tab concealing the tab of his zipper. With a quick tug towards her own body, Nicole released the button. Then, she pulled his zipper down, but only a fraction of an inch.

Nicole stood upright and, stepping back a bit, placed her hands on Jared's chest, and pushed him away from her with what seemed like a comfortable amount of force. "Lie down on the bed," she commanded, still managing to maintain her composure.

Jared glanced at the bed, a smile in his eyes, as he positioned the left side of his body towards the middle of the bed and then rolled over onto the flat on his back. He hadn't said a word, hadn't made any sound at all, but Nicole could see that he was on board with this sudden change of direction.

She unlaced his shiny Brogues and threw them on the floor, one at a time, each throw resulting in a satisfying hit against the wooden floor. Removing two lengths of rope from her purse, Nicole set them down on the dresser as she raised Jared's right arm up over his head, bending the elbow and positioning his wrist within tying distance of the bedpost. Not too loose, not too tight; and then the other one.

Standing near the head of the bed, Nicole looked down at Jared's long, slender body stretched out right to the footboard. She smiled inwardly, knowing that he was unable to touch her with his hands.

Sitting down on the side of the bed, Nicole removed her shoes and placed them on the floor. In the dimly-lit room, she slowly removed her dress, enjoying the tease at her own pace, under her own direction. Being in control lent a feeling of safety to Nicole. *Okay, I think I can handle this.*

Back at The Elaine, Jared helped Nicole out of the car and, reaching into his pocket, he removed a small box. Opening the lid, he displayed a large emerald pendant on a gold chain, which glistened in the light of the street lamp. "An emerald necklace would look stunning on that long, porcelain neck of yours."

As he latched the necklace behind her neck, he stood back to admire Nicole, intrigued by her youth and beauty. As if that wasn't enough of an enticement for Jared, he was now unexpectedly captivated by her feistiness and take-charge demeanor, not something Jared was used to in a woman.

"Why, thank you, Jared. That's so sweet." And she gave him a quick kiss on the lips. "But please don't think that you can buy my affection." And she tilted her head towards her right shoulder, looking directly into his turquoise eyes.

"I wouldn't dream of it," Jared smiled.

As they kissed goodnight one last time, Nicole imagined a father-daughter role-play.

Closing the door and turning the lock, Nicole tried not to wake Colleen. Nicole did minimal preparation for bed, and tucked herself in, wondering, *What the hell just happened?*

INTRIGUED

NICOLE SLEPT IN UNTIL TEN A.M. THE NEXT DAY AND, EVEN though it had been promised, she was still surprised when Kendra Howard's office called to set up an appointment that very day. Since the meeting with Kendra wasn't until one, she had plenty of time to choose the right outfit and figure out how to get to the campus.

Sitting up in bed, she was amused by replaying details of the night before; yet, in the light of day, it seemed more like a dream than reality. But a nightmare it was not.

Regardless of Jared's true motives, Nicole couldn't deny her excitement about the possibilities of what lay ahead. She'd be able to keep her apartment and establish herself as a resident of one of the most beautiful cities she'd ever seen. Whatever else might be included in the mix, and where it might lead, provided a level of intrigue that Nicole had not yet experienced.

One thing she knew: she would wear her classic grey suit, white blouse, and silver earrings. Stylish, practical, professional-looking, but not anything to outshine Kendra Howard. Nicole couldn't wait to see what the day would reveal.

Outside, a strong wind threatened to blow off hats, sweep papers down the street, and cause people to zip up their hoodies. With a spring in her step, as she headed towards the bus stop on the way to her job interview, Nicole noticed a beggar on the street corner.

Reaching into her wallet for a twenty-dollar-bill, thinking she'd help improve his life for at least one day, she withdrew the twenty, causing a fifty-dollar-bill to dislodge and blow away in the wind.

Even though the day was dark and gloomy, Nicole noticed a patch of light on the horizon. She heard a clap of thunder quickly followed by a startlingly close bolt of lightning cutting through the sky. Rain poured down in sheets as she took a seat at the head of the bus.

Want to know what happens to Nicole after this? THE TROUBLEMAKERS, A New Adult Novel, is available through Amazon and all major bookstores.

ABOUT THE AUTHOR

JD Monk is a retired chiropractor and teacher living in B.C., Canada. Her creative nature, passion for reading and writing, and inherent desire to connect with others compelled her to write this book.

www.marenhill.com/

STAY CONNECTED!

Join JD Monk's Tiktok page here:

- ♪ @chirodoc567
- ❏ @JDMonk
- ▢ @DrjdMonk
- ▢ @jdmonk
- ▥ @DrJudithMonk

.

Manufactured by Amazon.ca
Bolton, ON

25740258R00044